THE GIBILOES ARE AT THE BEGINNING OF
THEIR LIFE'S JOURNEY...

...AHEAD OF THEM THERE ARE MANY
TRIALS ON THE ISLAND OF DARKNESS.

The Island of Darkness

Linda Broom

Published in the United Kingdom by Jem Authors Agency

First Printed June 2023

Content copyright © Linda Broom 2023

A CIP record of this book is available from the British Library.

ISBN: 979-885-023-3723

www.jemauthorsagency.com

Dedication

This book is dedicated to my devoted husband, David James Broom. Always by my side.

I am honoured and proud that David chose me to be his wife and for his never-ending devotional care and support; a marriage made in Heaven.

And to our children, Lisa and Lyndon, who taught me more than they will ever know. My unconditional love for you both grows daily. I am so proud of the beautiful people you have become.

Also to our five grandchildren: James, Anna, Beth, Alice and Imogen; you completed our lives with so much love, fun and happiness.

The Gibiloes (pronounced Jib-i-lows) were invented by David for his grandchildren and they still remain a precious and special part within their hearts.

Acknowledgements

I would like to give my thanks to the amazingly talented Aileen Kraus from Germany, for taking the time to produce such beautiful illustrations for this book as well as for her special friendship.

I am grateful to my friend Matthew Facey of Mevagissey for his beautiful photographs that add such richness to these pages.

I am also thankful to Michael Thame and Jo Price at Jem Authors Agency.

In particular I'd like to thank Michael, author of the Conyers Street Mysteries, for his editing, support and guidance; I'll always be deeply grateful, and for Jo's efforts in bringing the pages to life.

Linda Broom

Contents

The Island of Darkness

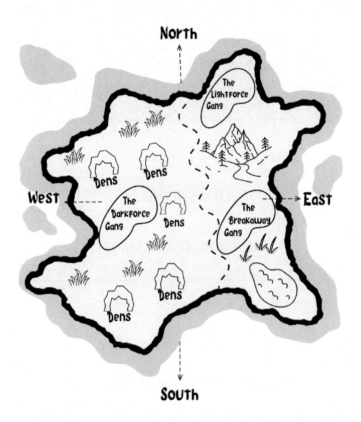

CHAPTER ONE

THE ISLAND OF DARKNESS

Aeons ago a meteor hit planet Earth. It landed on an island of

the Inner World known as the Island of Darkness and it was

so bad even the dinosaurs became extinct. Out of the

devastation some very scary, very angry and very dark and

badly behaved creatures emerged, and they are called

'Gibiloes' (Jib-i-Lows).

12

The Island of Darkness is deep under the sea and it's a very dark, desolate and creepy place. It is here, in this terrifying world, that the Gibiloes begin their fight for survival.

The island is one of a mini archipelago of seven islands, not that you can visit them. You can't even see them. What makes these islands unique is that they are deep under the sea in a place known as the Inner World. On the Island of Darkness, survival is a daily struggle.

The Gibiloes are at the beginning of their life's journey, a low form entity and the lowest in the creature kingdom, they have a dark, bad and dense energy permeating their fragile bodies.

And they have no idea what they should do.

But they must do something and, quickly or not, some of them learn the error of their ways and develop and progress to other islands in the quest to reach Enlightenment Island.

As they do so, so more Gibiloes appear. The cycle continues forever on the Island of Darkness, with each new creature beginning as the lowest form of life in the animal kingdom.

They don't start well. There is a dark, dense energy about them, not quite visible to the naked eye, but you can certainly feel it. It means they don't know how to behave or react to anything. They have no idea about life itself.

Ahead of them there are many trials on the Island of Darkness. To begin with, all they know is hostility and a place that no one would want to be. They don't know it, but it's all they can do just to survive.

Slowly they begin to grow and as they grow their inner vibrations change ever so slightly from the lowest frequency possible. Every Gibiloe feels it. And their survival depends on their ability to react. It depends upon their determination to overcome their darkness, their anger, and their bad behaviour to allow them to proceed and live on a better island.

Only the strongest of them will survive the traumatic ordeals that await them and, if they are not successful in this lifetime, then they reincarnate and return again and again until they pass all the tests on the Island of Darkness.

Thankfully most of them manage during only one of their lifetimes. And that depends purely on how they overcome the challenges they face and the actions they take whilst living on the island.

There is nothing nice, cheerful or good about this dreary place. Everywhere there is darkness, and very little light seems to be able to penetrate the strange web surrounding the island, preventing the healing rays of the sun to shine on this desolate land. Or them.

There isn't too much in the way of water or animals or plants or fruit trees or grasses. In fact, there isn't very much of anything that we might take for granted on planet Earth. Large areas are desolate and what pockets of food and water there are, are scattered around and not easy to find. The land isn't thriving, the plants and food sources are dying, and the oceans that surround them no longer seem to have any life left in them. The sea is the colour of sludge, and the rotting flesh of fish wash up on to the dry land.

No Gibiloe on the Island of Darkness has what we would call a home; they make dens, but they have to move often to keep on top of everything, because they have so much work to do.

Not only that, but the atmosphere itself feels cold and dark and miserable as it weighs heavily on the shoulders of these scared, bedraggled, and messy-looking creatures. Many don't even look as though they have the strength to overcome being knocked down by a feather let alone survive to live another day.

But survive they must, for this island is the most destructive, angry, and scariest of all the seven islands that Gibiloes live on. The life frequencies are at their lowest and, in reality, they are only just existing. That is no existence at all.

A Gibiloe sat on a small rock bewildered at what she saw. Nearby another Gibiloe kicked at a fish carcass and was sick as the smell reached his nose. They looked at each other, and the sudden realisation hit them like a thunderbolt; they were all alone on this beach and they didn't know how they got there. What could they do? They knew this was only the beginning of their nightmares and fear spread throughout their little bodies. This was the beginning of their first day of survival.

In the immediate area a few more Gibiloes appeared, stumbling around, lost. Others couldn't move at all and some just moaned and groaned. But the two of them began to explore the land they found themselves in, seeking a way out of the nightmare.

Black clouds began to rumble, the sea tossed and roared as the wind shrieked and one thing became clear to even the most dumbstruck of the Gibiloes; they needed shelter. They were desperately hungry, and their thirst scoured their throats, but without shelter, they knew they might not survive the impending storm.

The girl Gibiloe, whose name was Sparki, spotted a dark space between the trees. She pointed in its direction and the boy Gibiloe, who was called Kazem, seemed to understand. Together they made their way towards it as quickly as they could and, just as they left the beach and entered the dead forest, they realised they were looking at a cave set deep into a rock face. They hurried in just as the full ferocity of the storm reached the land and the cries of less fortunate Gibiloes carried on the whistling wind. Kazem took a deep breath as he listened to the horrors outside. Sparki sat further back in the cave and, for the first time, Kazem noticed she had a kind of aura about her? Something he felt but couldn't see. He realised he felt safer when he was closer to her, and he shuffled a little nearer. She seemed shy, but very intelligent. He didn't know why he was having these thoughts, but he knew he was never going to leave her side.

CHAPTER TWO

GIBIOLIATH AND TERRAMORE

Once the storm had passed, Sparki and Kazem went back to the beach and searched together to source what food they could nearby. Everywhere they looked there was devastation and still no sign of any other Gibiloes. Neither said anything, but Sparki did think to herself that other Gibiloes must exist somewhere.

Turning their backs to the sea, they ventured further inland. The devastation was not quite so bad as they made their way deeper into the forest, and Sparki found some coconuts that had fallen during the winds. She saw one broken on a rock, showing its brilliant white flesh inside and was amazed by the sweet taste when she licked at it. Soon Kazem, who was very shy and had hardly ever spoken started to smash another coconut on a rock, to split it open and allow him to taste some of the sweet juice that flowed out.

They were enjoying themselves so much that they didn't hear the rustling in the undergrowth until, suddenly, another Gibiloe stood in front of them. He seemed bigger than they were, and stronger and, before long, even more Gibiloes appeared, all bigger than Sparki and Kazem, but all looking incredibly hungry as well.

Kazem realised what was happening, and it frightened him a little; the other Gibiloes wanted to join them, and he realised they were looking for safety in numbers. Before long, there were dozens, all smashing coconuts as if they had just been taught how to forage for food for the first time.

As the group got bigger and bigger, two of the largest Gibiloes walked towards Sparki and Kazem.

"MY NAME IS GIBIOLIATH!" Said the first one. He was ferocious looking and very ugly, with large bulging eyes in his red face. His teeth were sharp, and two of them hung down like fangs over his chin. He didn't seem to be able to talk normally; he bellowed and his whole body seemed to shake with rage. His fur was matted and straggly and wafted around in the breeze.

"AND I'M TERRAMORE," shouted the second.

"YOU NEED TO COME WITH US IF YOU WANT TO SURVIVE!"

This one also looked ferocious.

All the Gibiloes had big swollen tummies because they were all so malnourished and hungry, but Terramore's tummy was even bigger and wobbled as he shouted and threw his arms about. His fur was so dirty it was impossible to tell if he even had any. He was almost completely bald apart from a few tufts that stuck out here and there.

Sparki looked at Kazem, who looked at the two terrifying Gibiloes in front of him and he tucked himself up close to her for protection before daring to speak.

23

"Okay," he said quietly, not sure why Gibioliath and Terramore seemed to be asking his permission. "Where are we going?"

Gibioliath and Terramore were definitely the strongest of the Gibiloes around. They were forceful yet seemed organised in what they needed to do.

"That way," Terramore said, pointing a three-digit paw deeper into the forest. "But first, we need supplies."

The order galvanised all of the Gibiloes, including Sparki and Kazem, and they picked up whatever they could to take with them. Some gathered coconuts, others fallen twigs for fire, some took grasses, not that anyone knew why.

But it was the only time all the Gibiloes seemed to have any life in them, and they all grabbed and snatched as they followed behind the larger forms of Gibioliath and Terramore.

They came to a clearing and everything was placed into the centre. Some Gibiloes rushed at the coconuts and started to try to smash them open. Others were forcing the flesh into their mouths before they had finished their previous mouthful.

Gibioliath stood up. "NOW LISTEN HERE," he bellowed.

"IF YOU ARE TO SURVIVE AND IF YOU KNOW WHAT IS GOOD FOR YOU, THEN YOU WILL DO AS WE SAY.

"MY NAME IS GIBIOLIATH AND THIS IS TERRAMORE. WE ARE YOUR LEADERS.

"SOME OF YOU WON'T SURVIVE, BUT IF YOU WANT TO THEN WE NEED TO GET TO WORK AND BEGIN TO BUILD SOME SHELTER!"

By now every Gibiloe stared open mouthed at the two largest Gibiloes yelling out orders. They were split up into small groups, so they were more easily controlled and given tasks to do but even that proved difficult for some.

Sparki and Kazem stayed close together, and watched in horror when a Gibiloe fell under the weight of work they were given to do, their tiny weak limbs twitching and trembling. Some were left where they fell, others were dragged towards the shelters by others.

It was a long dark cold gloomy day, and it got no better that first night. The silence was only broken by the cries of the Gibiloes as they tried to understand where they were, what would become of them. A lot of them huddled together for warmth and comfort as they tried to snuggle down and get some much-needed sleep.

The next few days passed horribly. There was fighting, arguments, lots of shouting, stealing and pillaging of the meagre food supplies in the other shelters. Everywhere unhappy bodies moaned in pain and desperation at their plight. Others lay lifeless as if their very life force was being drawn from their bodies. Even the land began to look as though it had lost its ability to renew itself.

Gibioliath knew he had to act otherwise Gibiloes would be extinct before they had any chance at life. He knew everyone was beginning to give up so he had to come up with a plan that would re-energise the group.

Many Gibiloes were trying to sleep, but Sparki and Kazem watched from their shelter as Gibioliath set off with Terramore. They were looking for a new area where plants, and therefore food, were more abundant.

Gibioliath pulled Terramore close and whispered as quietly as he could: "If we can get one group to work this area at least we will have food. We can take another group and they can start experimenting with seeds and stuff. Make some plants."

Terramore grunted. "Make some plants? You can't do that."

Gibioliath ignored him. "Others can collect supplies to strengthen our habitat. And we'll split them all into groups, ten at the most, make sure none of them get too strong."

Terramore grunted again. "Sounds like a good idea. There'll be loads of groups, but none as strong as us."

Gibioliath's mouth turned into a black, toothy grin. "We'd best get back in camp before they all wake up."

Sparki turned to Kazem. They had heard everything, and they didn't like the sound of it one bit.

"We need to get out of here," Sparki whispered to Kazem's vigorous nodding. They weren't sure how they would do it, or when, but Sparki knew they would have to leave as soon as possible because she did not like what she had seen.

CHAPTER THREE

THE TERROR BEGINS

As more Gibiloes woke up, so a hum in the camp became louder.

It was the sound of the surviving Gibiloes moaning or crying

under the weight of their misery. Once Gibioliath stood up and

shouted his plan no Gibiloe was still asleep. Even with Terramore standing next to him, glaring, the plan fell on deaf ears; they were all too weak and felt defeated.

Gibioliath began to get very angry, stomping around banging on anything that would make a din. Terramore followed and began to pull some of the Gibiloes out of the shelters, grabbing at their tufts of hair and twisting arms and legs.

"YOU WILL BE SPLIT INTO GROUPS," Terramore growled as he pushed defenceless Gibiloes towards one group or another.

Most didn't have the energy to complain even though they often fell and grazed their skin on the rough ground.

"DO AS HE SAYS," Gibioliath roared, spittle gathering at the corner of his mouth. "YOU'VE GOT TO GET TO WORK. YOU'VE GOT TO SEARCH FOR MORE FOOD!"

His menacing bulk lumbered towards one terrified group. They all stepped back as he towered over them. Gibioliath stared at them for a moment then pointed down a path through the trees. "That way, and don't you slouch."

The Gibiloes stood still for a moment, unsure what to do.

"MOVE!" Gibioliath screamed.

"M-O-V-E-!" he screamed again, and the group hurried away as quickly as it could.

Terramore had hold of one limp Gibiloe as he surveyed three similarly sized groups in front of him. He held up the lifeless body by one of its legs.

"IF YOU DON'T WANNA END UP LIKE 'IM, YOU'D BETTER DO AS YOU'RE TOLD! GO AND GET SOME FIREWOOD!"

A Gibiloe in one of the groups collapsed. It was enough to send all of the groups scurrying off in different directions.

"I'll BE WATCHING," Terramore shouted after them.

Sparki and Kazem watched on, terrified. Sparki, who was brighter than most of the others had a plan.

She grabbed a few Gibiloes as they stared at what Gibioliath and Terramore were doing, and pushed them towards Kazem, who understood and pulled at a couple himself. Soon they were a group of ten.

"Listen," Sparki whispered. "We've got to go and look as though we're doing something before they attack us. We must pretend to be working otherwise we'll never be able to escape. Come with me now."

Most of the Gibiloes understood, although one or two looked blank.

"Quick before they see us," Kazem said, hoping neither of the bigger Gibiloes had seen them.

The group moved off towards the forest; one thing neither Sparki or Kazem knew was where they were going; they just needed to get away from the clearing and the two monstrous characters in it.

"WHERE D'YA FINK YOU'RE GOING?"
roared Terramore.

The group stopped dead and slowly turned around. Sparki and Kazem were now at the back of their group and felt lucky for a moment as Terramore grabbed at the nearest Gibiloe, one that said his name was Bean. The terrified creature whimpered as the vice-like grip intensified on his arm so much that Bean thought his bones might break.

"You lot are stayin' 'ere," Terramore said, a fury seemingly danced behind his eyes. "I didn't say you'd be going anywhere, did I?"

Bean tried not to cry out but shook his head in a desperate bid to appease the giant Gibiloe squeezing his arm. There was a crack. Everyone heard it, then a bloodcurdling scream. Terramore flung Bean to one side. The poor Gibiloe held on to his arm as he smashed into the ground. He whimpered once, then fell silent. Terramore didn't even look but continued to stare at the now nine Gibiloes before him.

"You're on diggin' duty. I want tunnels dug so we got somewhere to put our food when it all comes from them others out there."

Sparki was first to move, with Kazem close behind and the others filing after them. Sparki walked in the direction Terramore was now pointing at and looked for the place he must mean he wanted digging. She fell to her knees and started to pull at the rough earth with her bare paws.

"We need to get out of here," she whispered to Kazem, who had fallen in beside her. "There's got to be a better way than this."

"I'M WATCHING YOU!" came a familiar roar from behind.

"I know," Kazem said. "But we've got to stay quiet. He's on to us."

Behind Sparki and Kazem's little group, Gibioliath and Terramore surveyed their work. All around them Gibiloes carried out their every whim of digging, fetching and carrying, supplying food dumps, making shelters, bringing and storing the firewood.

Occasionally they would go out and check on the foraging parties, but no-one ran away; every Gibiloe was terrified of their masters who thought nothing of hurling one of their number against a tree trunk or large boulder if they decided they weren't working hard enough.

As the days went on, the Gibiloes became weaker. Once one of them realised they could use the wings on their backs and fly up to treetops to get fruit, they all started to fly. Gibioliath quickly banned many groups from doing any flying, instead deciding on specialist groups that could, while the rest remained on the ground where it was easier to keep track of them.

The specialist teams that did fly got to the food more quickly and the stores grew in size, but many of them got weaker and weaker and some of them fell to the ground, twitching and scratching, trying to find any grubs they could eat or water they could drink to keep their strength. Some fell and never stirred again.

The tragedy that none of them knew was that Gibioliath and Terramore was too big to fly; any Gibiloe with any strength left in them could have simply flown away. None of them did.

Instead, the Gibiloes started to fight amongst themselves turning against each other, they kept stealing each other's meagre food supplies. Bullying of the weaker ones became an everyday occurrence, anger and destruction became the way of life. Things were getting out of control as their sadness, frustration and jealousy got worse.

Sparki and Kazem managed to stay strong, and their group was better behaved than all the others. Gibioliath and Terramore had been too stupid to notice this. Instead, they started to develop their own gang, so it became the largest and fiercest and was full of horrible Gibiloes who preferred to be bullies. They were all so dark and angry and had nothing to lose.

They became more and more violent towards the other groups and thought nothing of torturing them, pulling

37

hair out by the roots and breaking limbs, slicing them with sharp stones and leaving their wounds open. The poor Gibiloes that were the weakest of all were the hardest hit and often left alone to die. It had become a race of survival, and only the fittest would make it.

Every night was the same; Gibioliath would hold court with Terramore and his other fierce cronies. Some of them would go off on patrol, desperately hoping to find a stray Gibiloe they could beat. Other Gibiloes in the camp liked the look of this strong group and tried to join. Some were allowed, others were beaten back.

"They never get cold," Kazem said, as he watched on from the shelter that he, Sparki and the others shivered in.

"But we get them their firewood," said one Gibiloe bitterly.

"We are hungry, yet we get them their food," another added.

38

"And we know why," Sparki, said, her jaw set firm. "Our day will come. We will get away from here and we will live a better life. I guarantee you that. Let's keep repeating, 'we must be strong, we must be patient!'" Sparki looked around at the blank faces. "Come on," she urged, "'we must be strong, we must be patient!' 'We must be strong; we must be patient!'"

The others finally understood and gently nodded their heads, mumbling Sparki's words under their fragile breaths. Their lives were miserable, but Sparki had promised them a better one, and this gave them hope.

She had become the leader of her little group and it had happened naturally; every one of them realised she was the brightest and bravest of them all. They trusted her to decide when they would escape. Kazem was her second-in-command and supported her without question. He kept so close to her, he was more like her shadow. Somewhere towards the back of the shelter, Bean whimpered. The group had tended to his broken arm, and it was healing, but they were putting themselves in danger even by doing that.

Another loud roar of laughter came from the other side of the camp. Gibioliath stood up to cheers from his cronies, and bellowed loudly, his voice seeming to ring throughout the island.

"I'VE DECIDED UPON A NAME FOR US! I'VE DECIDED WE ARE GOING TO BE CALLED THE DARKFORCE GANG, AND I AM THE LEADER OF YOU ALL!"

Howls of laughter and shrieks of agreement filled the night air. Terramore had risen and put an arm around Gibioliath. The other Gibiloes all around, as far as the eye could see, whooped their joy and delight. Some danced around the huge fire other Gibiloes would have to replenish in the morning. Across the clearing Sparki brushed away a tear with her paw.

Kazem saw this and placed an arm around her shoulders.

Willow sat on the other side of her and did the same.

"I will get us out," Sparki whispered.

CHAPTER FOUR

BULLYING AND THE DARKFORCE GANG

The misery continued. None of the Gibiloes knew how long they had been in the camps ruled by Gibioliath, his had definitely become the largest gang of all, with more wanting to join them. He preferred to keep the strongest most horrible ones closest to him.

It could have been a few days, but it may have been weeks or months. None of them knew as they were so disoriented, their only thoughts being about survival and getting rid of the weakest Gibiloes.

Sparki and Kazem spent much of their time making sure their gang was safe and understood that one day they would leave. They knew that at some point Gibioliath's large gang would make a mistake. They were hoping it might be soon, but Kazem secretly worried they would die before that hopeful day arrived.

The numbers in Gibioliath's gang began to swell. Already the biggest group by far, Together they were the most volatile, ferocious and terrifying gang of all, thriving on bullying and destruction and control. Their energies were constantly at the lowest and darkest level possible and never fluctuated to be any lighter.

The other groups did have fluctuations in their vibrational energy levels, which meant they had moments of reflection where they could consider their actions.

The total darkness that had engulfed their spirits, lightened a little so that they could see the dull heaviness and frightening darkness that permeated

Gibioliath's and Terramore's gang. Most could feel it;

they only needed to be in the vicinity of one of them to

feel the change in the vibrations in the air as it became

a heavy dull sensation and their levels of fear and

anxiety increased.

And it wasn't just a sense of fear; some of the Gibiloes became quite ill when they got too close to a Gibiloe from that main gang. They would shake uncontrollably and pull at their fur in anxiety, some were even sick or became breathless at the mere thought of what was to come next. Sparki noticed all of these things as she was vigilant in the signs her group exhibited.

Gibioliath's gang laughed at the other groups when they saw them suffering, shaking, afraid and thought this behaviour was funny. They didn't need much encouragement, but some of them actively tried even harder to bully them; the more a Gibiloe reacted and trembled, the more enjoyable and fun they thought it was.

As his gang continued to pick on and fight the other groups, so they failed to notice a change was

45

happening and the groups were moving further away from the main camp. Sparki's group was the first to move way and, with each passing day, they moved a little further again. Gibioliath and Terramore had no fear as they ruled the island, as they knew every other group was smaller and weaker than them. No-one dared stand up to them when they were told what to do.

*

Another morning rose as the first shafts of grey began to light the camp. The Gibiloes who had guarded the camp overnight returned to their dens. At the same time other gang members were making their way to Gibioliath's den. It was a large dug out tunnel under a small hill and hidden from sight by shrubs, it was the most elaborate and concealed den of all.

As with every morning, Gibioliath began by bellowing his orders to everyone.

"Big day today, gang," Gibioliath said. "I wants us to get a load more food and wood, and I knows we've got to make them other Gibiloes work hard. Don't be shy; if you sees one of 'em not pulling 'is weight, hit 'im.

"IF HE DON'T CHANGE, HIT 'IM 'ARDER TIL HE DOES!"

The assembled Gibiloes needed no encouragement. They laughed as Gibioliath gave them their instructions.

The truth was most of them would have spent all day hitting other Gibiloes anyway.

"Don't forget to pick up any branches or rocks we can use for later," Terramore added. "You know, so we can have us another night of terror!"

At this the laughter grew louder. Every one of them was black inside. There was no vibration, nothing that showed pity or compassion or honesty. They were just evil.

One brave Gibiloe dared to ask Terramore: "Are we doin' this every day, boss? You know, keep 'em worried before we attack 'em?"

Terramore looked at the Gibiloe who had spoken, glaring at him for asking questions when he should simply follow instructions. Those around knew this had annoyed him.

"We needs to maintain a large amount of ammo at all times to ensure our own protection," he said through gritted teeth. "You can attack 'em whenever you wants. They're easily overcome."

*

With that the Gibiloes from the nearby camps scurried about picking up branches, long thick twine and any rocks they could use as missiles. They brought them back into the main camp and divided up the rocks so they all had roughly the same number that they placed into sacks and carried on their shoulders. It meant they had free paws to carry the sticks that had been sharpened into spears.

Gibioliath looked around, satisfied that his gang was ready to begin their march. As one large group they stomped around the island shouting hissing and banging on the rocks, their faces all scrunched up in anger, their eyes looking as though they would pop out of their heads. Hissing and shouting, sprays of their spit showered anyone nearby or brave enough to peer out from the dens.

Sparki had learned to hide when the rampaging began, but not in their den as it was too obvious. Her gang flew up and hid in a tree nearby, hidden by the branches. She had noticed that Gibioliath and Terramore were stupid as well as monsters, and they never seemed to look up. The biggest danger was the dark, heavy and frightful energy of this very large and wild main gang; when they prowled as a group, their bad energy grew heavier and the other Gibiloes that had moved camps further away could feel it dragging them down and making them more worried than usual. Sparki became increasingly anxious, looking at her gang as Gibioliath neared. She knew they could all feel this very dark, dense energy, but none of the others were as affected by it as she was. Now it was her greatest fear one of them would be so overcome, that they would panic and fall out of the tree.

Kazem saw Sparki looking worried and nodded back at her. Bean did the same. She knew at that moment that all of her gang were going to be fine as they all got comfort and strength knowing that they were looking after each other.

The noise didn't stop, and it was enough to terrify and panic anyone, but then the relentless bullying began. Gibioliath and Terramore grabbed the legs of two Gibiloes and began twisting them.

"C'MON! TELL US WHERE YOUR FOOD STASH IS!" Terramore growled.

51

But neither answered, so there was more twisting and tugging at their legs.

"TELL US NOW OR WE'LL CUT A LEG OFF!" Gibioliath roared, all the while continuing to shout and snarl.

By now every Gibiloe in the vicinity was watching what might happen next as the two were captured. They tried not to scream but the pain was so much that they had to. Despite the danger, nearby Gibiloes crawled out of their dens to see what was happening, and the air began to fill with panicked gasps.

"Stop it! Stop it! You are bullies, that's all you are! Bullies!" Everyone, including Gibioliath and Terramore turned to look at the Gibiloe who had screamed at them. She was called Teacup and she was the smallest and frailest looking of all the Gibiloes on the island, so she was being extremely brave. Sparki was impressed by her. All of her little gang were.

"What you gonna do about it?" Gibioliath laughed.

"GO AWAY!" Terramore laughed.

"WE'LL DO WHAT WE WANT, WHEN WE WANT, UNTIL WE GET WHAT WE WANT!"

Terramore shrieked the same words over and over again as Gibioliath tightened his grip on his captured and frightened Gibiloe until they couldn't bear it any longer.

"Our food is hidden under those rocks," he said. "Take it and leave us alone."

Gibioliath stopped snarling and dropped him on his head with a sickening thud.

"What did you say?" the Darkforce leader demanded.

"There is food under that mound of rocks," Teacup said, as she looked at the dazed Gibiloe on the floor and wanted desperately to help him. She had been dropped on her head by Gibioliath before and she knew he wouldn't stop until he got what he wanted; more food supplies and anything else he fancied taking.

A few of his gang ran forward throwing rocks or sticks into the air, not caring who they hit or where they landed, and pulled at the rocks hiding the food. They took as much as they could carry and ran back to the main camp.

The others rampaged on looking to find more Gibiloes to bully and frighten, it wasn't long before they came upon a small group huddled together at the back of their den, desperately hoping they wouldn't be found and bullied today.

Terramore's hand reached in and tugged at the first leg he found, dragging a terrified Gibiloe out into the open.

"WHAT HAVE YOU GOT FOR ME TODAY?" he yelled.

"Nothing!" the quivering Gibiloe called Pulsar said. "I haven't got anything."

"DON'T YOU LIE TO ME! WHAT HAVE YOU GOT?"

Terramore began prodding and pulling at tufts of hair. By now Pulsar was so frightened he began to wet himself, and all the Darkforce Gang saw it and began to laugh and point. Pulsar began to cry, and they laughed even harder. The bully held Pulsar aloft so that everyone could see his misery.

"THIS IS WHAT WE DO. WE WILL FRIGHTEN YOU; WE WILL INTIMIDATE YOU AND YOU UNTIL WE 'URT YOU AND YOU'RE BEGGING US TO STOP. IT MAKES US HAPPY TO SEE YOU SQUIRMING!"

"I really don't have anything," Pulsar managed to say between sobs. "Please let me go. Terramore released his grip on Pulsar, but before he had chance to try to escape a rope was tied around his body and he began to be dragged away.

"If you ain't got nuffink," Terramore said, "then you is coming wiv us to work in our main camp." The others dare not get out of the den, except for Bonnie, a feisty Gibiloe who looked so much like Pulsar that she was convinced they were twins.

"Where are you taking my brother?" she demanded trying to sound as brave as she could. The Darkforce Gang turned around as one.

"WHO D'YOU FINK YOU ARE?"

Terramore snarled.

"I'm Bonnie," she blurted out. More laughter echoed all around, Gibioliath even pretended to hold his sides in.

"Ha, ha, ha!" He laughed. "But you're not so bonnie are you? Look at you. You're ugly. There's nothing of you."

"And you're too skinny," howled another Darkforce bully.

"Jus' look at yer," said Terramore. "You can't even stand still. What's wrong with you?"

The teasing continued and despite her best efforts even Bonnie began to cry. Terramore started to poke her with the sharp end of his stick.

"Not so brave now," he said as Bonnie tried to fend off the spear thrusts.

So, the bullying continued, name calling, teasing, embarrassing anyone and everyone. Bonnie tried to stand firm, but the bullying was incessant, and her tears continued. Terramore grabbed her and began to tie her up too.

"YOU CAN COME WIV US TOO, AND DO WHATEVER WE TELL YOU TO DO!"

Bonnie was terrified, but it was what she had wanted; it meant she was going to the same place as Pulsar and that meant he wasn't alone. She wanted to scream for help, but she knew no one would come and try to rescue them.

As they marched away, the Darkforce Gang continued to laugh at Bonnie, calling her names and hitting her with their sticks. She exchanged glances with Pulsar who managed a weak smile, grateful that Bonnie was with him, wherever they were going.

As the Darkforce gang were on their way back to the main camp still shouting and banging anything in sight they came across a group they'd not really taken much notice of before.

They were sat out in the open and stared at the group marching before them, as they eyed each other Gibioliath instantly got angry and snarled because the group didn't move or seem intimidated.

"DO YOU KNOW WHO WE ARE?" he yelled. "WE RULE THIS ISLAND AND ALL THE GIBILOES ON IT THAT INCLUDES YOU, SO YOU WILL DO AS WE COMMAND!"

Eventually a tall Gibiloe called Teemo, who was obviously the leader of this brave gang because he stepped forward, upright, and the others filed behind him. He had never met Gibioliath or Terramore before, but he had heard all about this main gang, he'd joined one or two rampages before but had kept his group at the back and out of the way. He was always puzzled at how he'd managed to escape Gibioliath's notice for so long.

"I know what you are," Teemo said loudly so everyone heard him. "You are all big, bad, awful bullies. You cannot even talk properly, yet you come here making lots of noises, smashing things and throwing rocks at us. We're not scared of you. You don't

60

intimidate me or any of my friends. You are big bad bullies who should go away and leave us alone."

Teemo stood where he was, paws on hips, daring Gibioliath to challenge him. Terramore looked uncertainly at his leader. Behind him the rest of the main gang wondered what would happen next. They were all now frightened at how Gibioliath would react and as it turned out rightly so.

Gibioliath's anger went off the scales as he yelled so loud even some of the most hardened in his gang jumped. The silence was oppressive, the air charged with toxic energies that it altered the vibrations all around and which they could all feel.

Many of them went rigid, their mouths wide open, a look of horror on their faces. No one had ever dared speak to him like that before and they wondered

what he would do next.

A second Gibiloe stood up from behind Teemo

and whispered in his ear. "Ssh! They will really hurt us all

or worse. Keep quiet! Apologise quickly before he comes

over here." But Teemo stood firm as he knew he had to

against bullies. He turned around to look at his gang.

"These bullies," he said, "they might be bigger

than you, they might beat you up, but you must never

back down from one because they will only keep doing

it. Look at them; they are not used to being challenged.

It throws them off guard and someone needs to stop

them, I'm not afraid and he knows it."

Gibioliath's gang looked on, scared. It was not a

feeling they were used to. Gibioliath sensed this and knew

he could lose them if he didn't act as a leader. He began to size up Teemo, who was taller than many of his gang, but still much shorter than himself, and walked purposely forward, throwing his spear down as he did.

Teemo braced himself, there was a huge scuffle and fight, but it was no contest; the much larger Gibiloe grabbed him and eventually pushed him to the ground and before Teemo could move Gibioliath stood above him and stamped on his chest. Then he kicked him and kicked him again this continued until Teemo had to yell out.

"Stop it," he screamed. "Stop it! You're hurting me!" Teemo was squirming, but he still tried to grab at Gibioliath to try to fell him. It was to no avail. But the stamping only got worse as Gibioliath's anger grew. Spittle formed at the corners of his mouth and sweat dripped down his face. Teemo continued to wriggle and scream as the blows rained down on him, blood began to trickle and one of his leg bones snapped with an audible crack.

None of Teemo's group intervened as a seething Gibioliath was a very scary sight and they feared for their own lives. He had now lost control of his actions and didn't stop until Terramore pulled him away. Gibioliath raised a clenched paw and was about to swing until he realised who had grabbed him.

They simply left Teemo moaning and mumbling, making no sense at all. He couldn't move either so HIS group cleaned him up as best they could and fashioned a splint out of the spear Gibioliath had thrown to the ground. They carefully carried him to his den and made him as comfortable as they could. All they could do now was hope Teemo would survive.

CHAPTER FIVE

HATRED, JEALOUSY, ANGER AND BAD BEHAVIOUR

The low vibrational energy all the Gibiloes emitted meant they couldn't help showing hatred jealousy and anger. Their bad behaviour meant they had no respect for anything or anyone, including themselves. They displayed all the negative emotions, hatred and jealousy was common amongst them as each of them wanted something the others had. They were envious if they thought another had more than them, which meant they thought it all the time and greedily wanted to steal what others had. Many of them wanted what Gibioliath had or at least thought he had.

Despite the incident with Teemo, Gibioliath and Terramore still had control of the Darkforce Gang, and with every passing day, their memories shortened until no one remembered how defeated Gibioliath had felt. Quickly they fell back into old habits but one Gibiloe in particular, wanted power. He wanted to take over from Gibioliath and make the Darkforce Gang his own.

His name was Horrorbags. He was cunning and wanted everything Gibioliath had: power, control, respect and everyone doing what he said. He was so jealous he could barely hide it but if he wanted control he knew he would need to lie more than usual. He wanted the other gang members to rise up and topple their leader so that he could become their ruler and order the others about.

He waited until Gibioliath and Terramore had gone out on patrol one day and then he started to whisper. First of all, he went to all the Gibiloes he considered below him, and his hot stinking breath carried his message to them. He told them he was a stronger leader and that they wouldn't need to fear him like they did with Gibioliath.

"I won't even bully you," he said to every Gibiloe he spoke to. But they all recoiled from his fetid breath; no one wanted to listen to him, and they didn't believe him. Horrorbags started to lose his patience and the swearing came out. It was clear he loved trying to intimidate Gibiloes just as much as Gibioliath and Terramore.

Horrorbags became angrier and his language worse as his pleas were ignored. I'll show them, he thought and went off to his den. The others he had spoken to had already forgotten him. They started to squabble over sticks or rocks or food or whatever any other Gibiloe had that could be theirs.

Horrorbags returned with a coiled rope in his paw.

"What's that?" a Gibiloe called out to him. It was the invitation Horrorbags wanted, and he lassoed her with his rope. She screamed as the lasso tightened, then Horrorbags spun around, slowly at first, forcing her to run around, tied to the rope. He spun faster, her little legs finding it harder to keep up. Stars appeared in her eyes, her ears rang like bells and then she fell.

"DO YOU THINK YOU CAN IGNORE ME?" he shouted, spittle beginning to collect on his chin.

"LOOK AT ME WHEN I'M TALKING TO YOU! WHY ARE YOU IGNORING ME? WHY DON'T YOU WANT ME AS RULER? WHAT'S SO SPECIAL ABOUT HIM, GIBIOLIATH?"

He stared at everyone in front of him and then down at the girl Gibiloe AT his feet. She was still trying to get her breath back. He waited and she realised he wanted an answer, but there had been so many questions.

"I didn't hear you," she stammered at last.

"YES, YOU DID! I SAW YOU LOOKING AT ME!" Horrorbags glared down at the stricken Gibiloe.

"WHAT'S WRONG WITH ME? YOU SHOULD LISTEN TO ME. IF I WAS GIBIOLIATH, WOULD YOU LISTEN TO ME? OF COURSE YOU WOULD."

The rope tightened as Horrorbags pulled on it.

"Please," she begged, "undo the rope. I can hardly breathe!" She was now gasping painful, shallow breaths.

In his anger, hatred, jealousy and desperation Horrorbags suddenly realised how tight the rope was. He was now sweating and realised he had gone too far, so he began to release his grip.

The Gibiloes that were gathered around began whispering to each other about how jealous he was of Gibioliath, and little giggles broke out amongst them as word began to spread. Some of them looked anxiously at Horrorbags hoping he had not overheard them, but it was too late.

"YOU'RE CRAZY!" He screamed.

"I'M NOT JEALOUS OF ANYONE! NO WAY AM I JEALOUS OF GIBIOLIATH!"

The Gibiloes cowered and, stupid as they were, they realised Horrorbags had no idea just how bad he looked. His face seemed to swell and redden as he pointed and poked.

"JEALOUS? WHY WOULD YOU SAY THAT? WHY?"

"We didn't say that," said one of the now cowered Gibiloes, nervously.

"Why would we say that?" spluttered another.

"We wouldn't say that would we?" said a third. "We were talking about ourselves, it's us we were talking about ourselves, it's us that are jealous of you."

"Is that right?" sneered Horrorbags looking around the group.

"Yes," they cried, almost as one.

"Yes," said another quickly. "We were talking about being jealous of you. We are all jealous of you, Horrorbags."

Horrorbags frowned, unsure what to think as he knew everyone in the Darkforce Gang was dishonest. None of them told the truth if they could get away with it. It was always violence, anger, theft, more violence and jealousy. Everyone was the same. They had hatred in their hearts, and it was what they thrived on. Lying was like breathing.

Horrorbags knew he had to be more cunning to win them over. "I've got a plan," he said, smiling. He tried to turn them against Gibioliath by saying he had let them down. "What has he achieved? We are all still fighting to survive and after all the destruction we've caused there's not much left. I will do a much better job and treat you well. Just give me this chance."

His pleas sounded desperate and too many of them didn't look impressed because they were far too frightened of what Gibioliath and Terramore would do to them if they betrayed them. Horrorbags was beginning to feel defeated and desperate, but his jealousy was so intense he continued telling lie after lie. He would soon learn that if you do anything for all the wrong reasons that it never works out. Fortunately for all the Darkforce gang he was interrupted by the sound of Gibioliath's return as his stamping noisy arrival was always the same as it echoed around the main camp.

Gibioliath raised his paw and silence fell upon all the assembled Gibiloes.

"Eat," he said as a huge bucketful of fruit was placed in the centre of the camp. "Eat now, because you must rest this afternoon. We've got a lot of preparation to do."

"What for?" asked one of the cheekier ones.

"For a long night of destruction!" proclaimed

Gibioliath. The Darkforce Gang cheered.

Horrorbags had slunk away.

CHAPTER SIX

THE WORST NIGHT

The night was black. It began like many others; Darkforce members wandering about camp working themselves up for the terror, fires crackling giving out the only light for there was not one star in the sky. The feeling was eerie, crackling with a bad terrifying and tense atmosphere as everyone realised something big was going to happen. The air was filled with tension and anxiety. This they knew was going to be unlike any other night and it made some of them fearful. Even the scariest, wildest bullyboy Gibiloes were worried for what the night held for them.

Gibioliath looked particularly evil and although he wasn't the largest of them, he had large bulging eyes, his mouth hung open and two fang-like teeth emerged that almost pierced his lips. His hair didn't blow in the breeze that was beginning to whip up, but instead stood in spikes on his furrowed head. His three-fingered paw had very sharp claws and one prod from them would leave a nasty gaping hole in a Gibiloe's flesh. He called the Darkforce Gang to attention.

"We must hunt down as many Gibiloes as we can especially the weakest ones, I want them to be frightened for their lives. I want their homes destroyed. Burn them out if you have to. Take all their food supplies; if they starve it means we won't."

The leader stood proud. His calls for violence always had the desired effect. But he could see some in front of him were shocked. The reality had hit; many Gibiloes could die tonight and the days ahead. Gibioliath became aware of the hesitation.

"WE HAVE NO OTHER CHOICE NOW,"
he bellowed.

"C'MON, WE HAVE TO DO IT IF WE ARE TO HAVE ENOUGH FOOD AND SUPPLIES FOR ALL OF US HERE NOW. IT'S SOMETHING WE MUST DO. FOOD SUPPLIES ARE AT THE LOWEST THEY'VE EVER BEEN THERE IS ONLY ENOUGH LEFT ON THE ISLAND TO FEED US, OTHERWISE ALL OF US WILL DIE."

He was lying. They had enough food, but Gibioliath was greedy. He was the greediest in the Darkforce Gang, and the most power-hungry.

He thought one way; that to stay in his position he must give his gang a purpose. He needed to keep them occupied. He needed to give them victories. He needed to reinstate his dominance after the incident with Teemo daring to challenge him.

And so, Gibioliath and Terramore secretly held a meeting and had a long discussion about what to do next.

The only way to appease his Main Gang was for violence to happen and Gibiloes to die. But they knew they couldn't go too far. Gibiloes could not become extinct, not that they knew why. They agreed on one thing; what was needed was the best night of violence ever!

Gibioliath let out his battle cry. Terramore screamed and howled. The rest of their gang joined in as they marched into the dark night, with fires being lit along the way, smoke billowing across the island, wood crackling with embers swirling into the air. the worst night the island had ever seen had just begun!

The usual noise was made, missiles were thrown randomly through the air and laughter followed if any hit their targets. Frightened Gibiloes ran from their dens and hiding places.

The main large Darkforce Gang gathered more of the smaller gangs along the way, knowing it was the weaker Gibiloes that they were going to destroy.

The howling, hissing and screeching continued, becoming unbearable for the weak and terrified ones cowering in their dens. They seemed to be aware this night was going to be more ferocious and horrific than ever before.

It wasn't too long before dozens of Gibiloes started to emerge, driven out by the smoke and the fear of fire burning them in their dens. The main gang members set upon them as soon as they appeared, and screams of their pain were added to the howls, as yet another poor Gibiloe succumbed.

Trees caught light and thuds were heard as Gibiloes who had used their wings to fly up and hide in the canopy fell to the ground.

Horrorbags roared his gang on, not caring that the fires were burning the food supplies as well. It didn't matter. Food could wait.

This was hatred, anger, violence and it was all that any of them wanted at that moment. By now the whole gang not only wanted it to be the worst night of violence the whole island had ever seen; they knew it was. They were now absolutely desperate and felt as though they had nothing to lose. The more Gibiloes they tortured and died, the more homes they destroyed, and the more destruction

they caused the happier they became.

"GIBIOLIATH COME LOOK AT THIS,"
Terramore shouted above the din. His leader approached,
face pulsing and eyes bulging.

"THERE'S A STASH OF FOOD BURIED
DEEP UNDER 'ERE. HELP ME SHIFT THIS
ROCK."

The rock moved easily revealing underneath a huge

stockpile of fruit and nuts and things the other Gibiloes had

hidden to survive.

"Someone bring a sack and get all this food,"

Terramore said, and a Weasley gang member hurried

forward, his eyes almost popping at the sight of all the

food. In that moment his only thought was to steal the

food for himself, but his face fell when Terramore

grabbed him and pulled his face close to his, distracting

his thoughts.

"AND DESTROY THEIR DEN WHEN YOU'VE GOT IT ALL!" he snarled.

Gibioliath had moved on. He was in his element.

He howled some more and began darting in and out of

the shrubs and from behind trees so that confused

Gibiloes never knew where he would spring from next.

"I RULE THIS ISLAND! THIS ISLAND IS MINE!" he shouted for the tenth time, and for the tenth time, the Darkforce Gang roared their approval.

"NO ONE DARES TO CROSS ME!" was met with another cheer.

But as Gibioliath and Terramore stole food,

Horrorbags continued to set fires and tried to smash as many

Gibiloes as he could with his stick. More dens were

destroyed and more weak Gibiloes were left out in the cold

with no food or shelter. It was known that none of them

would survive.

Further afield, a long way from the main camp, one group of Gibiloes was waiting for them. They had made spears and daggers from the trees around them, they had stones that they had previously sharpened, and they were ready for a fight as they had learnt that on some occasions you had to stand up to these mad bullies and retaliate. They had remembered and learned that from the very night before when Teemo had been cruelly attacked after he had been so brave to stand up to bullying, showing them how they must react. Well, they were fighting for their survival now.

Gibioliath was first, then Terramore, then the rest of their gang crashed out of the forest into a wide area of grassland. Ahead of them twenty or thirty Gibiloes stood in a line, each armed, some carrying flaming torches and all looking very determined. The very sight of them standing together daring to look menacing angered both Gibioliath and Terramore. Once the initial shock of seeing anyone dare to stand up to them, they started to shout insults, and scream about what they would do to them.

Then Gibioliath screamed, "CHARGE!"

They clashed, they shouted, they brawled, sticks banged together, rocks smashing all around them and the screams became almost unbearable. They pulled each other to the ground and rolled about banging heads on nearby rocks, smashing heads on the hard ground and even slashing arms and legs with their homemade daggers. The air was heavy with the cries of the injured; the stench of burnt fur where flaming torches had caught a Gibiloe. The injured from both sides lay rolling in pain and screaming.

As the fight continued, Horrorbags's group sought out new dens to burn, new hideouts to turn into infernos and smoking ruins. His gang lay in wait for Gibiloes to come spluttering out of their hiding places, the smoke burning their lungs and making them cough uncontrollably. They were dragged, punched, hit with sticks and Horrorbags smiled. He was doing better than Gibioliath; he was sure of it.

*

It had been the worst night yet. The air was thick with smoke. Gibioliath took a moment from smashing heads to look around at the carnage. Gibiloes, both from his gang and their opponents, lay groaning. He wasn't clever, but he had been on the island so long that he understood the horrors, the violence, and the injuries were necessary. He just had to make sure it kept getting worse.

He loved the bad behaviour, the hatred, the jealousy and the anger. They all did. Fear, destruction, dark miserable desolate lands, a lack of food and desperation meant the Island of Darkness was the most hostile environment the Gibiloes would ever know. He had made it hostile enough for the night.

84

Finally, the extreme levels of violence and brutality could stop. He called out. "GANG, WE HAVE DONE ENOUGH! THE NIGHT OF VIOLENCE CAN END. WE WILL BE BACK. OUR EXISTENCE DEPENDS ON IT!"

"YES!" Terramore roared in response.

"ENOUGH FOR TONIGHT! LEAVE THE WEAK AND INJURED. THEY'RE NOT STRONG ENOUGH TO SURVIVE. BUT GRAB SOME OF THEM STRONGER ONES; WE WILL NEED THEM TO WORK AROUND OUR MAIN CAMP."

Gibioliath's group headed back into the forest and scythed at anything they thought resembled a hiding place or den. Gibiloes ran out, some were captured, and the amount of smoke caused by Horrorbags hurt everyone's eyes. Any Gibiloes caught in their path were taken, tied up and dragged back to Gibioliath's stronghold. As they marched back to camp, they all jeered and laughed at their plight.

The captured ones were past caring what happened to them now. All they could think about were the ones left behind and how many, if any, of their friends would survive.

At last, the gang reached home. Gibioliath walked slowly to his den as his minions tied up what prisoners they had and headed to their own dens. It had been the worst night of violence yet, and they had all enjoyed it, perhaps a bit too much. Now they were all exhausted and Horrorbags watched on as everyone headed back to their own dens, leaving the captured ones out in the cold night air with only leaves to lie on. A long silence once again fell upon the battered island.

Horrorbags smiled.

CHAPTER SEVEN

THE CLEAR UP

The following day left them worn out from the previous night, so they all stayed around the camp. Most slept much longer than usual while others were restless and aimlessly wandered about, a few of them taunting their captives.

Some would wake up, their stomachs rumbling because they wanted food, and then they would have to find it seeing as their own camp was such a mess after they came back last night.

Eventually a lot of the main gang congregated together and decided to see the destruction for themselves, so off they ventured to the previous night's area of carnage not only to begin to clear up but hopefully replenish supplies, if any could be found.

But they were in for a shock as there was destruction

and ruins and little smouldering fires everywhere, with a lot

of land totally destroyed. Lying around were hundreds of

missiles, spears and the bodies of Gibiloes too weak to

survive the onslaught, their dried blood turning the colour of

the soil a rusty brown.

Rolo now appeared on the scene. He was the oldest

on the Island of Darkness and he lived quietly away from any of the gangs as he liked to be on his own. He had been watching the previous night's rampage but kept well out of sight. He had survived this island for a long time and had loads of experience. He had developed techniques to help him cope, mainly by ignoring everything he'd seen and done and not dwelling on any of it.

His little body had become toughened and scarred over time, and his arms and legs had grown wrinkly. He was so skinny because he was constantly starving. He walked with a lopsided limp from previous injuries he'd sustained in the many fights he'd endured, which was why he always carried a wooden stick. He had removed the bark from it, so it was bright and glossy with a carved-out circle at the top.

His eyes were sunken but still had the spark of survival within them. This is why he had decided he wanted to help as many Gibiloes as possible escape the Darkforce gang. He wanted to get them further East where he knew there that was a better-behaved group of Gibiloes that had already escaped and were so far out they were left undiscovered. They were called the Breakaway Gang.

Gibioliath and Terramore knew Rolo was not a threat and the only one who lived by himself. So, they left him alone as he was no threat to them and he wasn't worth their time or effort. The gang carried on looking for supplies and clearing away the debris, putting out some fires.

But there was no food and no sign of life, just a bare burnt-out long stretch of land.

While he had kept out of sight, watching them trying to clear up, Rolo had spotted a smaller group of Gibiloes at the back busily working away collecting missiles. He was fascinated by them as they seemed distant from the main gang and kept themselves to themselves. He watched them for a long time before he went up to them and introduced himself.

"Hello," said Sparki in response. "We have to appear as though we're working, but we're looking for an opportunity to escape as my small group have had enough of all this hatred and torment." She didn't quite know why she was telling Rolo all this, but she felt she could trust him.

"Ha!" Rolo said, quietly. "It must be your lucky day because I have helped other Gibiloes escape. There's a group further East from here, called the Breakaway Gang, and they welcome Gibiloes like you to their group.

"Once you've had enough of the torment you begin to develop a conscience, just like you are now. You also begin to feel so weighed down by these bad dark energies it makes you feel ill just thinking about doing anything bad to another Gibiloe. It means that your vibrational energy is increasing its frequency and if you don't escape you will not survive as you need to be around those that feel, think and act like you."

Sparki realised she and a few others had stopped

working. She looked over to where Gibioliath and Terramore

were talking to each other. It didn't look as though they had

noticed.

"Walk away," she said in a loud whisper. "Please stop talking to us; we are being watched." Sparki bowed her head and began clearing away debris into a pile. The others in her group did the same.

"Don't worry, I have a plan," Rolo said grinning as he rubbed his chin. "All I need to know is how many outside your gang would be suitable to join us."

"That's easy," Sparki said, without looking up. "There's ten in my group, ten in Teemo's and I'd like Bonnie and Pulsar to come too, but they're tied up at main camp."

Rolo seriously expressed the need to keep things quiet and not to breathe a word even to each other about any planned escape; their lives depended upon it.

He started to help clear up, but he stayed very close to Sparki so they could talk. To any of the other watching Darkforce Gang it looked as though there was nothing out of the ordinary. He hatched a plan with Sparki and immediately started planning.

Sparki managed to get word to Teemo once Rolo had left and their two small groups carried on with the clear up, putting out the fires that remained and collecting any spears and missiles they could use. Rolo had left instruction that once the main gang were ready to set off back to camp that Sparki's and Teemo's groups should linger behind until the main gang was out of sight of them.

The clear up took most of the day. They left with what little they could salvage, but it was obvious that the burnt and destroyed land would take many years to recover, that's if it ever did. Certainly, no Gibiloe could survive there, nor would they want to. Many had lost their lives that night and the ones that couldn't be saved were left where they fell. A few at least were buried under burnt out bits of wood.

"RIGHT! YOU LOT LETS GET GOING!" bellowed Terramore.

"WE NEED TO BE BACK AT CAMP BEFORE NIGHTFALL. THERE'S NOT MUCH MORE WE CAN DO HERE NOW. WE'VE CERTAINLY GUTTED THE PLACE."

The gang immediately hauled their bits onto their backs and began marching off back towards home, thrilled with the ruins they'd left behind.

Sparki's and Teemo's gang slowly and carefully began to draw back, gradually distancing themselves from the main group, desperate not to draw attention to themselves. It was difficult to keep calm as the tension and panic rose within them. They knew they had to remain silent and calm. Their lives depended on it.

Terramore and rest of the main gang were so happy about their own achievements they didn't notice any of the Gibiloes had gone missing. Although there had been loads of clearing up to do, compared to their night of violence it had

been an easy day for them. Many crashed into their dens and

went straight to sleep, not even bothering to eat.

They slept until late the next day.

CHAPTER EIGHT

THE BREAKAWAY GANG

Early that evening, Rolo once again met up with Sparki's and Teemo's gangs.

"We need to prepare for a battle from the Darkforce Gang as soon as they realise you're missing," he said, rubbing his chin. "They'll be outraged and won't stop looking until they find you. I'm going to ask some of the Breakaway Gang to help us stop you being re-captured as we need a lot more help to prepare a barricade. These attacks are getting worse, and we need to be able to defend ourselves. If there's only us, they'll just pick us off one by one, I reckon."

Before long Rolo had a large army of volunteers arrive and he began to delegate with a flip of his paw – how many would work on this and who would go with who. He'd done it many times before, although perhaps not on this scale.

"Now gang, let's get cracking," he said. "We need to do this quickly in case the Darkforce Gang are awake. If they're not already on the way, it won't be long before they get here."

Rolo had given everyone specific tasks to complete then he waved his paw in the air, the signal for everyone to get working. So, a hastened scurry of about fifty Gibiloes sped off in all different directions and began working on keeping the main Darkforce Gang out.

A large trench was dug that stretched from the north of the island to the south. It was covered by ropes and debris, so it didn't look like a trench. The idea was that the Darkforce Gang wouldn't notice and would fall straight into it. A second trench was dug behind the first and filled with rubbish that would quickly burn, creating an impenetrable barrier, ensuring the Breakaway Gang could safely escort

their new members back to their camp.

They had only just managed to get it all done when

they heard the stomping and roaring of Gibioliath's lot. It was

the same as it ever was, lots of shouting and yelling and

throwing of missiles and more screaming as they came out of

the forest and crossed the burnt ground to get at the missing

gibiloes. They were so blinded by their rage that many of

them fell straight into the first trench.

99

Their howls of hatred quickly became howls of confusion as they struggled to get free from the ropes, or climb out of the trench. Teemo took this as his cue and he lit the fire in the second trench, flames soon flying skywards. It was impossible to attempt to get through. The first of the Darkforce Gang to escape the first trench were beaten back by the heat from the second.

This was the only time the Darkforce Gang had ever retreated and Terramore informed Gibioliath that the ones that had escaped weren't even worth trying to capture.

"JUST LET 'EM GO!" He yelled.

"WE DON'T NEED 'EM, THERE'S MORE THAN ENOUGH OF US! THEY WON'T SURVIVE LONG HERE. LOOK AT THE PLACE; IT'S DESTROYED WITH NO FOOD. LET THEM DIE!"

Gibioliath was furious but knew what Terramore said made sense.

"BACK!" he shouted over the sounds of cracking wood and the roar of fire. Confused Darkforce members turned and tried to scramble up the other side of the first trench and away from the flames.

Rolo knew there was no way the Darkforce gang would try to follow them so far East after the humiliation of being defeated and they wouldn't even bother to come this far out again. They were too lazy and probably would be glad that they had less mouths to feed.

Now Sparki, Kazem, Teemo and all the others were free to go and live a more peaceful life with the Breakaway Gang and learn a better way of living. Rolo's job was over for now and he returned alone to his den happy and content that once again he had successfully helped to relocate Gibiloes. That was his only mission in life.

On their arrival at the Breakaway Gang's camp the newcomers were warmly welcomed by everyone and so many questions were being fired at them. But they couldn't reply; they were speechless at what had happened to them. They didn't know what freedom was and they seemed to be in a trance-like state trying to take everything in.

It was to be expected as the shock and trauma of what they had all suffered in the past confused them. Looking around they could see lots of food and improved dens, but it was the strange feelings that overcame them by being in this calmer, quiet place that shocked them the most. At first the relaxed atmosphere made them feel uneasy and unsure.

"This is going to take some getting used to," Kazem said quietly as they wandered around in a daze, unable to take in what was happening to them. They were not only safe, but free from deprivation.

Eventually they were ushered to an area under cover that looked like an open shelter for it was here all the Gibiloes of the Breakaway Gang gathered to eat every meal together. The evening passed quickly as the newcomers began to relax, the questions and answers went back and forth.

Varg was the leader of this gang, he was respected and proud quietly spoken and had a calming presence about him, but he was very firm in dealing with his group. There was no way he would allow any shouting or bad behaviour towards each other or any of the destructive traits they had previously known. Each morning he held lessons that everyone had to attend and practice sessions on the benefits of good behaviour were regularly held too.

He needed to ensure that newcomers felt that they weren't expected to get everything right and to know they would make mistakes, but they must not worry as no punishments were given.

"Here we all aim to help each other," he explained, "and we understand that some will learn more quickly than others. But there will be no embarrassing those that need extra help. There will be no shouting, bullying, fighting, violence or destruction, none. Do you all understand?"

The newcomers nodded in agreement. Teemo stepped forwards. "Don't worry," he said. "We've all been through too much and none of us liked doing those awful things, but we were too afraid not to obey.

"We had already been feeling something in us was beginning to alter. We could sense it, but we didn't know what it was or what to do about it."

"Everything around us," Varg replied, "all those material things, all the plants trees, food and each one of us vibrates at different frequencies. This is all energy.

"Bad behaviour, destruction, hatred, jealousy, anger, violence are all resonating in the lower dark, dense energy field. Living amongst Gibiloes like that keeps your own energy at the same low vibrational frequency level, which is why it's difficult to get away from.

"Once you all began to feel differently and behave differently your own vibrational energy increased in frequency too, that's why you gravitated towards each other. Like attracts like."

"Ah!" Sparki said. "I understand better now. That's why we needed to keep our distance and why we always trailed behind. That's why we felt differently!"

"That's it," Varg said. "You'll learn more in the following days, but for now get some rest. Please try to sleep. "We have prepared dens and beds for you all. Goodnight."

"Goodnight," they whispered back.

*

Sparki found it hard to take it all in. She snuggled down into her bed feeling safe for the first time she could remember.

But then she had a thought, and it was about Bonnie and Pulsar being tied up in that awful frightening camp. She found herself trying to come up with a plan to rescue them and bring them here and to safety.

But it had been a long, hard few days and she was exhausted, so she put the thought to the back of her head to try and get some much-needed sleep. As she was drifting off her thoughts went once again to Bonnie and Pulsar, and she couldn't get them out of her mind. She only settled when she had decided that Rolo would be the one that could help her get them released. With that thought she was soon snoozing soundly.

Whilst the new Gibiloes settled into the Breakaway Gang and were learning how they lived in this part of the island without a thought of being destroyed by the Darkforce Gang, life began to peacefully settle down.

Following a few days of rest and recuperation the newcomer group was beginning to relax and enjoy their new-found freedom. They couldn't wait for the morning's lessons to start, and they didn't need to be called to attend as they were already there, waiting for Varg to arrive.

"I'm impressed with how keen you are to learn and very happy that each day you are all up ready and waiting for me!" Varg said, gazing upon the Gibiloes seated before him. "Have any of you noticed how different you feel and behave?"

Little paws waved in the air. "Yes! Yes, we have!"

"I feel more relaxed, calm even," another excitedly chatted on. "I haven't worried about anything for days. I feel happier and excited now and I want to learn all you can teach us."

Why are we helping each other more, and why haven't we been nasty to anyone?" Sparki asked. It was something that still confused her.

"Because you've long since left the Darkforce Gang behind with all the bad and dark negative energies they emitted and encompassed you all in," Varg said. "We all want to be more likeable and become better Gibiloes. We developed a conscience too which meant if we were to return to those bad habits it would make us feel unhappy, regretful, irritable and that would start to make us feel ill.

"You've already developed a conscience and are concerned about helping each other, caring for us all even though you don't know us that well at the moment. Once you are amongst others doing the same kind and good things, your energy vibrates at a higher level of frequency and the energy between everyone remains high and stable, which is why you all feel happy, protected and safe.

"Mix with good Gibiloes and you are also doing good, mix with bad Gibiloes you also do bad things. We are emerging from the dark into the light."

Weeks passed in the Breakaway camp without too many incidences but then one evening Teemo, inexplicably, began to panic and became irritable. His voice began to rise and, before long, an argument had occurred with several of the gang joining in.

Gibiloe after Gibiloe started to shout at each other. The argument was beginning to get out of control, but they didn't know how to stop it. Arms and paws began waving about and the noise got louder.

Varg had been watching the scenario unfold and had been waiting to see if they could resolve it for themselves. After all, they'd spent a long time learning about behaviour and that should have helped them.

But he knew he had to intervene so, very quietly, he walked up to the offending Gibiloes and without saying a word looked at them and stood very still. He calmly put his paw up and got their attention.

"Ssh!" he whispered. "Ssh! What seems to be the problem? Let's all take a breath and calm down."

They were so shocked at his politeness, kindness and the quietness of his question that silence immediately fell all around. They looked at one another with embarrassment across their faces, realising their error. Heads hung low and no one could speak for a little while.

"Oh! My goodness," Teemo said, breaking the silence. "I'm so sorry. I don't know what came over me. I began to raise my voice because I disagreed with something someone said and before I knew what was happening, I was screaming."

"It's okay, calm down, relax," Varg said. "Take a few deep breaths. No one is expecting you to be perfect, none of us gets everything right all the time, but can you see how quickly your feelings and energy changed?"

Teemo ashamedly had to agree with a nod of his head. Varg looked at all of the assembled Gibiloes and said,

"What I want you all to realise is that nothing is ever achieved or resolved by shouting or arguing. Nothing. That's because when you stop listening, you don't actually hear what is being said. You've lost control of your own thoughts and rationality and if things escalate, well, you all know what happens then... all the bad energies begin to take over, don't they?"

"Yes, they do," Sparki said immediately. "Our vibrational energy will drop because that energy is lower in frequency. So, if it continued, fighting would break out and that's the sort of behaviour we've left behind."

"Well said, Sparki!" several of them chimed in unison.

"Please try and remember this experience and learn from it," Varg said, a smile breaking out on his face. "Remember, it's much better to get your point across in a calm way and, more importantly, listen before reacting. As soon as you begin shouting you've lost the argument. You've made yourself feel worse; it really isn't worth it. Always be the better Gibiloe.

"The same reaction would occur if you were jealous of what any other Gibiloe had. The feelings grow so strong, it would always be on your mind and the only person to suffer is you. Always feel and be thankful for what you have. If you want more, then you have to work hard to achieve it for yourself, like you have all done to get here. It was hard for you, but so worth it.

"And it's exactly the same when your anger and hatred burns deep inside you. All of those dark and dense energies consume you, that makes it difficult to overcome those feelings, especially when you're surrounded by everyone else feeling the same way."

By now, several more Gibiloes had come to listen to Varg speak. He had an amazing and calm way of talking that instantly engaged his audience.

"You must remember the lessons you're learning here and if any of those thoughts of feelings should rear their ugly heads, remember you will be the one that suffers the most if you don't get away from it or keep it under control.

"Work hard and practice forgiveness. But forgiveness doesn't mean you are letting those that have caused you trauma or their bad behaviour off the hook; it means you are no longer going to let it concern you or worry you. You're leaving it all behind. And behind you is the only place it should be. That way you will find peace within yourself.

"Once you've understood the traumatic experiences and why you've had them, then thinking of others and helping them is an excellent way to continue to heal and keep yourself well, happy and in control."

A Gibiloe let out a little sob. Varg's words had been beautiful, and he had given them all a wonderful lesson without even trying. The atmosphere was electric; Gibiloes were bursting with happiness as they all felt the surging increase of positive energy.

*

The next day began as every other but there was excitement buzzing around the camp with whispers spreading about someone new joining them in the Breakaway Gang. They were gathered around for morning lessons as Varg approached with several others following. In the middle stood Bonnie and Pulsar. Sparki was elated and ran to hug them, tears of joy running down her little face, she was soon joined by the others for a large group hug.

Varg didn't want to break up this lovely, happy sight, but he had to be very serious for a moment. "Please listen carefully," he said, immediately capturing everyone's attention. "I don't want anyone asking any questions of how Rolo and I managed this rescue. Bonnie and Pulsar have been through a lot, and they need your care and love. No one should remind them of what has happened. All that matters is everyone is safe. They will now join us for lessons.

The day proceeded as any other. After lessons they spent their time doing positive things. Sparki and Kazem talked to Bonnie and Pulsar explaining how things worked and sometimes giggling a little at their old friends as they tried to understand just how different the Breakaway camp was. But as Varg had asked, neither of them spoke about what had happened when they had been rescued. Bonnie in particular seemed to grow taller as the day went on, her confidence and spirit helping her to rise from the depths she had been in.

After the evening meal, whilst everyone was gathered together in the same place, Varg had a very important announcement to make. There was tension brewing in the air. Bonnie and Pulsar's return had been a huge event, but now there seemed to be more.

"Many of you will be leaving here soon," Varg began. Gasps could be heard all around. He pointed a paw to a mountain range in the distance, burnished orange by the setting sun. "Over those mountains there is another group of Gibiloes called the Lightforce Gang. Only a few of us are aware of them. They are more advanced than us and they continue training all you Gibiloes that have passed your lessons whilst here with us.

"There you will learn lots of new techniques to enable your growth and development. But for those of you who will be going, and how you get there, that will be for another day."

CHAPTER NINE

PREPARING TO MEET THE LIGHTFORCE GANG

A few weeks later, Varg had called a meeting which left a buzz all around the camp as most of them felt sure they knew what it would be about.

"Tonight," he began, somehow sounding even softer and calmer than normal, "I firstly want you all to know how proud I am of all your hard work, but it is now time that a lot of you need to move on. You have outgrown all that can be taught here."

All the Gibiloes looked happy but worried at the same time. No one was sure if they would all stay together. Varg continued without interruption. Three-quarters of the breakaway gang that had had been there for a while were leaving and they gathered to Varg's right.

"Sparki," he then said, "you and six of your group will join them. Teemo, you and six more of your group will also join them." Varg noticed the gasps and looks of fear on their faces and quickly continued. "Please don't worry or get upset if you're not chosen this time. It means you will remain here with me and continue with lessons until it's time for you to leave too.

No one spoke but continued to watch Varg as he wandered about everyone and gently tapped the top of some of their heads. When he did so he would quietly say, "Please join the group preparing to go."

Bonnie and Pulsar were two of the ones being left behind there were tears, but at least they knew they would be safe. Sparki understood but she was still sad to move on without them.

"Please get your things together and say your goodbyes," Varg said. "We don't want this to be long and drawn out; it must be done. You will all be together one day

in the future, so hold on to that thought, always."

Varg led the way east towards to the mountain range

where they would camp up to await the arrival of a Gibiloe

called Powa from the Lightforce Gang.

*

Behind the high ridge of mountains there was less than a

quarter of the island split off from the rest. The ridge was

impenetrable to enemies, the sun shone for long periods of

time, and the food was wide ranging and plentiful.

Everything looked luscious, the plants and shrubs were

flourishing, and the sea was much clearer. Several different

types of fish could be seen swimming around.

The Gibiloes that lived here were called the

Lightforce Gang because they had long since left the low and

dense dark energies behind and were living a much more

thoughtful and productive way of life. The vibrational energy

119

they emitted was of a much higher frequency than that of any other Gibiloe living on the Island of Darkness.

Powa and Towa were the main Gibiloes that looked after the Lightforce Gang and their environment, but everyone here worked together as they were all anxious to progress to a higher level in their development. Powa was slightly taller than her group and she had a more delicate appearance about her than Towa. She also had an immense inner strength, elegance and intelligence. Her pretty, delicate face was a sight to behold; her perfect dark round eyes were mesmerising and seemed to emit love from them. She was the only one trusted enough to have secret meetings with the overall Ruler of all seven islands of the Inner World that Gibiloes lived on. His name was Jeremiah Ess the oldest Gibiloe to have ever lived. At the moment Towa was the only other one aware of these meetings and the existence of the other islands.

Powa had taken some of her group to the high mountainous ridge that separated them from the Breakaway Gang and, further afield, the Darkforce Gang. Once at the foot of the range a number of little Gibiloes gasped and their mouths fell open.

They all seemed to speak at once, "Powa, there's no way we can fly or climb over those mountains, how can we ever get over them?"

"Don't worry my friends," Powa smiled. "We are not going over we are going through."

With that Powa raised both her paws in the air and pushed against a crooked crack in the rocks above her head. Slowly after creaks and groans and odd little noises a doorway opened up and they could all see a long dark tunnel ahead of them.

"Follow me," said Powa and quickly but quietly they all filed into the dark tunnel. Once at the other end Powa again raised her arms into the air pushed against a long and crooked crack in the rocks to open another secret doorway that revealed a bit more light, although it was still pretty grim and dull compared to the light they were used to.

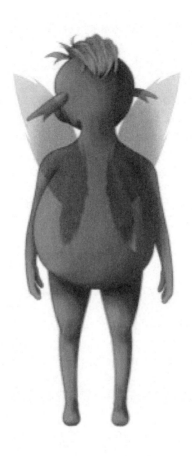

Waiting to greet them on the other side was a large

group of Gibiloes that were leaving the Breakaway Gang to

become part of the Lightforce Gang.

Without any fuss or much ado Powa quickly and

quietly led the new Gibiloes back through the tunnel and had them all march forward so they could see their new home

and meet the rest of the Lightforce Gang. They all followed

her instructions and, in what seemed like the blink of an eye,

the mountain doorway closed behind them, and they found

themselves in the safety of the Lightforce Gang.

A few days had past while they tried to adjust to this

new environment. It was a bit of a shock to have so much

light and food. They needed to acclimatise and recover their

energy, so they spent a lot of time sleeping, being totally at

ease. No one was rushed. it was left to them when they

wanted to explore their new home and meet some of the

new gang. On their fourth day a meeting was called so that

all of the Lightforce gang were together as one new group.

"Let us all welcome our new friends to our gang,"

Towa said. "Welcome! Welcome! We have lots of work to

do. Are you ready?" The newcomers looked shy and were so

quiet no one heard their replies. Towa repeated her call and in unison Lightforce Gang old and new loudly said they were ready.

Powa took over, "It is our duty and desire to help you raise your vibration to a higher frequency than it is now, and you must do so before you can move off this island never to look back."

The newcomers gasped in delight. Other Islands! None of them had any idea of this.

"There are six other islands after this one," Powa continued. "The next one is Mischief Island. As you know a bit about energy, frequency and vibration here you will expand on that and learn techniques like breathing, relaxation meditation, visualisation positivity and mental strength."

The Gibiloes listened intently, and you could hear a pin drop. Powa's soothing voice was the only sound that broke the silence.

125

"First let me explain about this energy and the best way to do that is to give you examples. Can you remember when you were with the Darkforce Gang, how dark, dull and sad you were?"

"I can," called out one Gibiloe sat close to Powa.

"Well, think about your time there. Think about the bullying, violence, hatred, and destruction happening every day, It caused your bodies energy to feel flat, low and miserable, didn't it?

"Dark bad energy was vibrating at the lowest of frequencies and being in that environment for long periods of time made you continue to do so many bad things. This is why so many of them couldn't learn how to behave, they were constantly in the dark, being dragged down by those around them.

"Now think about the time you made friends with the Gibiloes from the Breakaway Gang. They began showing

126

you that there was a better way to live, that you could learn to help each other and begin to behave without all the bullying and bad behaviour."

All the Gibiloes nodded as one.

"Yes, Powa," said one, eagerly. "We can remember that we began to feel safer and more cared about."

"I felt better within myself too," another said. "I wanted to be and act like the Breakaway Gang and as soon as I started doing some good things, I felt lighter and happier. I actually felt the dark and dense energy being left behind and I liked this lighter vibrational energy that was increasing my frequency."

They all agreed no one wanted to go back to the darkness and dark ways now they were all excited and keen to learn even more. They could remember a saying from the breakaway gang; 'out of the darkness into the light'. That's what they wanted to learn more about.

The next day Powa took a small group to learn a bit more about it. "Although this is all new to you," she said, "and maybe you don't quite understand it at the moment, you will. It will be so powerful that it helps you to ascend to such higher levels of being you will wonder how you could even have survived those bad dark moments.

"I will give you enough knowledge to enable you to move on to the next island. It's a continual growth and development of your life soul and spirit. Sometimes you will find it repetitive but it's essential to grasp it until it becomes a natural instinct built into you.

"Your mental strength is possibly your best tactic in overcoming any adversity, remember energy follows thought. So, if in your own mind you can convince yourself you can do something and really want to do it, you shall overcome your fears and it will be accomplished. If you hesitate and think Oh no! I cannot do that, then you set in motion that energy thought out into the universe that you cannot do it. Energy follows thought!

"So, my question is, what happens then?"

"One little paw went up, "you won't be able to do it."

"Correct!" said Powa. "Now that is a very brief and basic example but is a good place to begin, let's do some work on those facts."

In another area of the new camp, Towa had a group of new Gibiloes sat around her in a circle. Once they were settled, she told them they were going to learn about visualisation. The group looked aghast. None of them had ever heard the word before and certainly didn't have a clue what it meant or what they were about to do.

"Yes," Towa continued. "Visualisation is one of our mind control techniques that we use and when worked alongside all the other strategies you will be learning over the next few

Things that LOWER your Vibration

💜 ANGER

💜 HATRED

💜 JEALOUSY

💜 BAD BEHAVIOUR

💜 GUILT

💜 ANXIETY

💜 WORRY

💜 NEGATIVITY

💜 FEAR

💜 RESENTMENT

💜 SADNESS

 LAZINESS

Things that RAISE your Vibration

 LOVE

 HAPPINESS

 KINDNESS

 MUSIC

 CARING

 POSITIVITY

 ENTHUSIASM

 GRATITUDE

 MEDITATION

 FORGIVENESS

 NATURE

 RELAXATION

months, it will help in not only saving your lives but will increase that vibrational energy we keep talking about. Combined they are the only way you will succeed in leaving this island."

Kazem was the first to quietly speak, almost in a whisper, as he raised his trembling paw, "Is that not too hard for us to do? I'm already feeling butterflies in my tummy."

"No Kazem," Towa replied in a soft and gentle tone. "It's not too difficult, but like everything new you've all learnt it takes practice and patience."

She walked amongst the group. "I need you all to get as comfortable as possible and relax. Breathe in through your noses and hold for ten seconds, then slowly breathe out through your mouth. I want you to do this for half an hour.

"If sounds around you interrupt your calm and relaxed mind, ignore them. Let them fly high up into the sky."

They all relaxed and began their breathing exercises, the surroundings seemed to slow down in time and was only interrupted by the quiet and calm voice of Towa. "You all know what the berries on the bushes look like, so now I need you to imagine in your mind's eye the size of the berry, the colour, the taste, the shape. Is it rough or smooth? Think of nothing else but those berries. Close your eyes and in the darkness of your mind's eye, as though you were looking with your real eyes wide open, see those berries, feel them touch them taste them until your mouth is watering.

"If any other thoughts pop in your mind, begin again and repeat the sequence. Please continue to do this for as long as it takes to successfully see, feel your berry and nothing else enters your mind."

For some it was easier than others but for a first try, Towa was impressed and knew that her praising them all would give them the encouragement they needed to proceed. Their first basic test on visualisation was completed they now had a foundation on which to build.

Towa quietened down her now excited chatty group. "That was the easy bit," she said. "We will go on to do more visualisations and they will gradually become more difficult. We have lots of time to practice."

And practice they did. The last words Towa uttered as their day ended stayed with them as they went to bed, "Remember, energy follows thought... if your energy is focused on the bad, bad it will remain. If you're focused on the good, with good thoughts that remains in your mind and body."

Energy follows thought!

Energy follows thought!

Energy follows thought!

*

The third group were beginning meditation and mindfulness sessions with a Gibiloe called Crysta who had such a shiny shimmering fur it almost glowed. Her tiny face always looked happy, and her smile was beautiful. Whoever encountered her couldn't help but smile back as her energy exuded with such joy and enthusiasm.

"Let's all get into comfortable positions," Crysta began, smiling at the assembled Gibiloes in front of her. "You can sit upright like me or lay down whichever you prefer. Now relax and let your arms flop by your side.

"Meditation is the practice of expelling all thoughts from your mind and transporting yourself into a safe beautiful space by visualising what or where you'd like to be.

"We'll begin by doing the breathing exercises slowly in and out, in and out until you're feeling relaxed safe and calm. Begin at your toes and imagine them relaxing so much they fall to the floor. Work your way up your feet then your legs, abdomen, chest and your head.

"Keep slowly doing small breaths until your whole body is relaxed and you can feel yourself almost floating away. Imagine the sun shining down on you and everywhere you look is beautiful and perfect. Stay relaxed. Now imagine what your life would be like if you lived there. What do you do? What is everyone else doing? Once you've done that, I want you to slowly remember where you are now and who you are with, slowly wiggle your toes then open your eyes."

Kazem couldn't wait to tell everyone what he experienced and before Crysta could stop him, he was off!

"I did it!" he said. "I actually did it. I went to the most beautiful place. It was so beautiful; I didn't want to leave. Even the Gibiloes there were so exquisitely beautiful. They were unbelievably caring and kind, loving and embracing, that none of it can be true!"

Crysta raised a paw to get everyone's attention and to calm Kazem down, who shook his head in continued disbelief at what had just happened.

"What Kazem has achieved is remarkable," she said. "But I can assure you all now, that what he meditated on is true. There is a place where the Gibiloes are exactly as he described." Crysta cleared her throat. "Now let's try another one. I want you to imagine that you are lying in a green and luscious field with no one else around. You can feel the warmth of the sun on you as it seems to snuggle around your body. Nearby you can hear the ripples of water gently lapping around the rocks in the stream. You begin to feel safe and more relaxed than ever before.

"You're not even sure if this is real or a dream. Keep seeing and feeling those sensations over and over and you'll begin to drift off into what feels like another world that you don't want to open your eyes and miss it all."

Crysta then snapped the fingers of one paw against the other, waking the Gibiloes with a start. None of them knew if they had been in this deep relaxed state for minutes hours or days.

Crysta smiled her beautiful smile, "I'm sorry to jolt you, but some of you were so relaxed it looked as though you'd drift off to sleep. It's nothing to worry about because in the early days of learning this technique everyone does it. It's not easy but we will persist."

One or two Gibiloes sighed, others tried to understand what had just happened to them, but as a group, they were tired. It was clear they were getting tired and restless, and Crysta had noticed it.

"That's it for today," she said kindly. "We will continue working on meditation and mindfulness another day as it will get harder and harder as we go deeper into our consciousness."

138

The days that followed were trials exercises and daily practice sessions, and each group had to do them all and pass them before they were allowed to move on to learn new things. Some got it very quickly whilst others struggled to keep their minds open but they all tried and persevered, no one was giving in but more importantly they were enjoying it. Months of practice ensued and the Gibiloes moved on to each of the group sessions to learn new skills until they had mastered them all.

And it was something that came to them naturally. They all persevered without complaint and enjoyed the work and lessons. For the first time they were beginning to feel happiness and contentment, and that they were worthwhile little Gibiloes.

It wasn't all work, practice and learning though; they also had lots of free time where they could chat, play around or simply go for long walks in the fresher air that blew over their camp towards the mountain range. The food was plentiful and nourishing and their fur was becoming thicker with a sheen to it, their stamina was also improved.

*

Then, one day, it was time for all of the Lightforce Gang to have a meeting to discuss progress and next things to do for their development.

"We have been watching your progress and seeing you all achieve so much," Towa said just before supper had begun. "Powa and I are overcome with gratitude for being among us working so hard. Well done! Very well done! None of you have shown signs of going back to your old dark ways, so now I'm delighted to pass you on to Powa for her to share some exciting news."

Powa rose from her seat to the sound of clapping and cheers, the sounds ringing in her ears as the atmosphere rose and the Gibiloes became more and more excitable and energised with happiness and expectation.

Powa raised her paw and silence fell.

"Tonight, you will meet the oldest and wisest Gibiloe ever to have lived. He rules all seven islands here, deep under the sea. His name his Jeremiah Ess and he is coming here to meet you. I know you will all show him the respect he deserves by standing upright and giving a nod of your head to welcome him once he arrives."

Unbeknown to every other Gibiloe on the Island of Darkness, Jeremiah Ess regularly visited all the islands and had secret meetings with their leaders. On this island, that was Powa. Just then there was something of a commotion at the back of the clearing.

Slowly the assembled Gibiloes split to make a

pathway down the middle of them. As Powa had asked,

every Gibiloe stood up straight and bowed their heads

slightly as Jeremiah Ess (for it could be no one else) slowly made his way towards Powa and Towa. Every single member of the Lightforce Gang was standing and gently bowing. It was a sight to behold and never forget.

He looked so graceful, proud and wise with his glasses perched on his nose.

Jeremiah Ess reached the front and gave a little bow of his own to Powa and Towa and then to the rest of the Gibiloes who all looked on in awe.

"Please, you may all sit," he said. "And thank you for a warm welcome." He turned to Powa and Towa. "You have done a wonderful job here and I think I will have a lot of Gibiloes that will be moving over on to Mischief Island. How many do you think have passed their trials?"

"I'm delighted to let you know that every single Gibiloe in my Lightforce Gang, even the newer arrivals from the Breakaway Gang, have all proven they are ready to move on." Powa could feel the love emanating from the gang as she spoke. "As discussed previously with you, however, I do need some to remain to help train the next new group that will be arriving later on."

"As so many will be leaving us tonight," Towa said, "Powa and I would like to suggest that one of us and several more should remain here to help train the next new group we will be receiving from the Breakaway Gang.

Jeremiah Ess stroked his chin and was deep in thought.

"Mm! Mm!" he murmured. "Let's get everyone together and over supper I think we'll ask for volunteers first as I've never taken so many Gibiloes to Mischief Island in one go before."

*

After the supper feast, the Lightforce Gang huddled around a little fire waiting to see who was going and who was staying.

They had all eagerly watched as Jeremiah Ess had whispered to Powa and Towa during the meal. Jeremiah Ess even spoke to Crysta to get her views. They did not have to wait long to find out what was going to happen...

"Well, my little Gibiloe friends," Jeremiah Ess began, "it's been wonderful to see you and I'm really proud of the work you've undertaken and even happier that none of you were lured back to the Darkforce Gang. Just look at you all, here amongst the Lightforce Gang, your progress is wonderful to see!"

The Gibiloes began to relax, and a joyous glee spread about their faces.

"You have done brilliantly!" Towa agreed. "But as you all know, we need some volunteers to stay behind to help with the next group of Gibiloes that escape the Darkforce Gang.

"Can I please see a show of paws of anyone prepared to stay."

A number of paws shot up straightaway and Powa was surprised and impressed. Little voices chimed, "I'll stay," or "I want to help." Sparki and Kazem also wanted to stay as they knew they'd meet up with Bonnie and Pulsar in the next group of arrivals.

Jerimiah Ess nodded his approval. Clearly this was an excellent group of very selfless Gibiloes.

"This is wonderful to see," he said. "I'm sure you won't need to remain for long but thank you all who have volunteered. It makes my task of not having to select any Gibiloe to stay much easier.

"Can all those who are not staying behind, get ready for the next journey in your short lives to Mischief Island. Gather your things and let's say goodbye to the ones staying behind."

Jerimiah Ess led the way towards the sea with Powa, Towa and Crysta following behind and the departing Gibiloes following on behind them. Those remaining skipped along with their friends to the beach excited to see how and from where they were going to be collected.

It was dark now, and the stars in the sky seemed brighter as they twinkled in the moonlight that was shimmering across the sea.

The waves began to grow in size and Teacup was the first to notice. "Look!" she yelled, pointing her paw out to sea. "Look out there! There's a really big wave coming! I can see something moving."

Jerimiah Ess laughed out loud.

"That, my friends, is Myrtle the turtle. That is how we all travel under the sea. She has special magical powers that ensures your safety. Once on board, you'll see my main Gibiloes from my Island of Enlightenment, which is where, hopefully, you will all end up.

"You will recognise them instantly because they have all dressed in beautiful clothing and each will be wearing a Golden Heart bracelet with their names on them, so you can easily identify them. Their names are Cheruby, Sweety Pie, Beauty Pie and Tinks. They will remain with you on Mischief Island until you've settled in.

"Once we get on the back of Myrtle you won't recall the journey but will awake refreshed and ready for your first day on Mischief Island!"

"Right!" Powa called out over the hubbub. "Come on everyone, single file, march on to Myrtle's back and settle down." One by one she counted them on board where

Cheruby, Sweety Pie, Beauty Pie and Tinks greeted them warmly with hugs.

Once everyone was snuggled together, they felt a small jolt and a funny sensation fell over them; they were off on their journey with no time to waste and they were asleep within seconds as Myrtle started to dive under the sea.

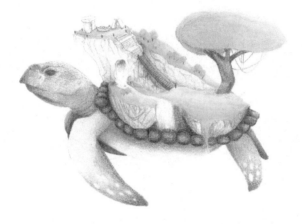

When they wake up, they will be on Mischief Island where another adventure awaits them. What do you think life be like for them on another island? What mischief will they get up to? Do you want to find out? Good! Let's follow the Gibiloes to Mischief Island...

The 7 Islands deep under the sea. Follow the Gibiloes journey from the dark to light

3 Island of Kindness

7 Island of Enlightenment

2 Island of Mischief

4 Island of Unconditional Love

6 Island of Healing

1 Island of Darkness

5 Island of Trials

If you would like your own little Gibiloe to take on your journey, please contact grannysays1@gmail.com, visit www.lindabauthor.co.uk, or look for me on Amazon.

Printed in Great Britain
by Amazon

26166792R00086